The
Storyteller
of
Ketu

CW00953306

Written by Chitra Soundar
Illustrated by Neha Rawat

Collins

2

Chapter 1

The village of Ketu was nestled in the valleys of vast mountains, under the canopy of banyan trees, beside a forest.

The people of Ketu were hardworking. They grew their own food. Their minds were full of imagination and their hearts were full of wonder about their mountains, the river and the woods that surrounded them. They imagined the world beyond too, where the river met the sea and the mountains touched the skies.

The village of Ketu was famous for its wonderful arts and crafts. The potters made jugs of unique shapes, with decorated handles. The weavers wove cotton saris and tunics that had unusual patterns and colours. The painters and the poets depicted beautiful scenes in their paintings and poems.

Every month, the artisans of Ketu crossed the river to the big town on the other side. People from other villages and towns flocked to buy their creations. Everyone admired the unique wares made by Ketu's talented artisans.

The artisans saw the beauty of nature and made it
come alive in their work. Indeed, the soil under their
feet made excellent clay. The cotton they grew was
perfect for weaving, and the reeds they gathered from
the river were suited for basket making.

They drew patterns of art by copying the constellations
of stars. They wrote poetry about the moon and its
travels. The art of Ketu was unique because the most
important ingredient they used was their imagination.

Their imagination was fed by the village storyteller. No one knew her real name. She was old, wise and full of stories. So they called her Kathakar, the storyteller.

When she was young, she travelled across the river and down the mountain to the great plains. She had seen winters that brought snow, summers that turned the lush ground into sand, and rains that lashed for weeks. But her favourite season was spring when new plants grew, flowers bloomed bright and the birds laid eggs in their nests. All the things she had seen, smelt, heard and felt, enriched her stories.

Kathakar spent her days exploring the forest surrounding Ketu. She listened to the birds sing and the grass rustle. She could tell from the clouds and the smell of the earth if the rains were going to come. She watched little birds learning to fly. She listened to frogs croaking in the shallow waters of their rock pools. She learnt the calls of the birds, whispers of the mice and the drumbeats of rain over the rocks.

Every evening, as the sun set, Kathakar sat under
the biggest banyan tree in Ketu and hummed a song.
That was her call to the people of the village to come
and listen to a story.

Kathakar's story was often set in the past, but it was
filled with smells, sounds and colours from their lives.

From the eldest in Ketu to babies, everyone was invited
and everyone came to listen. It was their nightly treat.
A time to wonder after a long day's hard work.

Chapter 2

The time when the sun slanted into dusk was the most beautiful time of the evening. That was when Kathakar told stories. Her stories had wisdom of the world.

"Ever wondered how day and night came to be?" she asked. "Let me tell you a story ..."

Long before the world turned into what it is today, there was no night. Just the brightness of day and the darkness of the forest. In a small hamlet like Ketu, a young man was chosen and sent into the deep forest every day to collect resin. Resin was neither a liquid like the river, nor was it solid like the land. It was the sweat of the trees, and the colour of trapped sunshine. Collecting and burning the resin was thanking the god of sun. One day, a young boy who was quite impatient was sent to the forest. He trekked through the trees looking for resin.

Soon he came upon a tree with resin. The boy climbed up to peel off the resin. Then he spotted a cricket sleeping in the hollow. He trapped the cricket in his palm and ran back home.

On his return, the elders were angry that he had not brought back any resin. He opened his palms and showed them the cricket.

"I found this," he said.

"Why did you bring it from the forest where it lives?" asked his mother. "Its family will be looking for it."

But the boy didn't care. He kept the cricket inside a coconut shell and didn't let it go. The cricket called all day and all evening, and the boy didn't pay attention.

As the cricket called, the sunshine went away. The village was drenched in a blanket of darkness. The people were afraid. The sun had brought them warmth. Now they were cold.

The elders appealed to the sun for mercy. They lit more resin to please the gods. But nothing worked.

"It's all the boy's fault!" the elders shouted.

"I didn't do anything wrong," the boy said.

The boy's mother realised that he hadn't yet understood what he had done wrong. She dragged him to the forest and left him in the darkness. The boy cried at first. Then he worried about the snakes and the stinging scorpions. He was lonely. Then he understood. The cricket would have been lonely too. He went back to the tree where he had found it and let it go. He watched the cricket join its family.

The boy kneeled on the forest floor and asked for
its forgiveness.

The next morning, the sun returned. The boy led
the village to offer thanks. But this time, the sun
didn't stay for long.

Everyone realised that this was the new way – a while of
darkness and a while of light to remind them that they
should treat the creatures of this world with love
and understanding.

After Kathakar finished her story, everyone talked about how they must protect the creatures they live with.

The potter said, "I imagine resin would glow like the sunset." Everyone agreed that Kathakar's stories were filled with wonder and wisdom.

Chapter 3

Kathakar told them a new story every night.
Every story lit up the people's imaginations.
Even the baby, whose house was closest to the banyan tree, listened carefully and imagined.

The baby had been listening to stories weeks before he was born, when he was inside his mother, who was listening to the storyteller. The stories soothed him and made him sleep peacefully at night. So his parents named him Gumaan, the one who imagines.

One evening as the sun set, the waxing moon was three days old. Kathakar settled down under her tree, humming a song gently. The villagers went on with their chores. They came to listen to the story reluctantly.

"We can't stay long," they said. "We must get ready for the big fair on full moon's day."

"Please keep the story short," said the potter. "We have lots of work to do."

Some were late. Some left early. They frequently interrupted the story with whispers and chatter. Their thoughts were elsewhere. But baby Gumaan was listening to every word as he rocked in the cradle that hung from the tree.

Kathakar was slightly annoyed. But she didn't
fuss too much. After all, big fairs excited everyone.
More people to buy things meant more money.

19

Each evening, the villagers were a bit later than the previous evening. Some stopped coming altogether.

"I need to finish the pots," said the potter. "I'll be back tomorrow."

"I just had an idea for a new painting," said the artist. "I'm going to work all night."

Even though the crowd thinned, Kathakar told her story as usual. Baby Gumaan was always there, his eyes wide open and ears alert to catch every word and every pause in the story.

The night before the big fair, everyone was excited.
The artisans of the village were bustling like bees
all day. That evening, no one had time for stories.

The villagers hurried and scurried. They packed
their wares in their carts and then settled in for
an early night.

Kathakar sat under the tree and waited. Gumaan lay in the cradle, humming to remind Kathakar to tell him a story. His mother had gone back into the house to work.

As the moon rose in the sky, Kathakar was left with just the baby.

"You're special," she said to Gumaan.

She whispered a story into Gumaan's ears. She told him about the potter's star-shaped vase, and the carpenter's toy that could fly like a bird. She told him the secret of the beautiful crafts of Ketu.

By the time his mother came to collect him, Gumaan had fallen asleep, his dreams full of stars and birds.

Soon after, Kathakar packed her bag and walked out of Ketu. As she passed the last house, she turned back with tears in her eyes and sadness in her heart. But she continued on, out of Ketu.

Chapter 4

Next morning, the sun shone bright. Everyone in Ketu was busy getting ready for the fair. Children were excited to watch clowns and acrobats, eat corn and groundnuts, and choose toys from other parts of the world.

At the fair, people from far and wide had come to buy things from the artisans of Ketu. Their hard work had paid off. The people of Ketu returned home, laden with riches.

That night after they returned home, the villagers decided to celebrate. They feasted and danced all night long. No one except Gumaan missed Kathakar, the storyteller. Baby Gumaan hummed the song he had learnt from her, over and over again. But no one paid any attention.

A few days later, the people of the village realised that the storyteller was gone. They missed her stories. But life went on without her, anyway. There was no time for stories and wondering about the universe, they thought. There was so much work to do. No one except Gumaan missed her stories.

But as days went by, the artisans, the poets and the artists had no interest in trying new patterns or designs. The carpenter didn't invent new toys. They made the same things, over and over again. Their pots and pans, poetry and paintings were called dull and boring after a few fairs had come and gone.

"I can't imagine how to make new shapes of pots," said the potter. "I can only make the usual ones."

"I can't imagine the colours of the sunset over
the mountains without going there," said the artist.
"And I've forgotten how to imagine new things
to draw."

The poet moaned too. "My poems are all about
the same thing, over and over again. No one wants
to listen to them anymore."

They had forgotten to stop and wonder, and imagine
things beyond what they could see. They were no
longer able to make beautiful things.

Except Gumaan who imagined stories on his own by
watching butterflies and birds.

"Ever since Kathakar left us, we've lost our ability to imagine," said one elder.

"We didn't have time for wonder," said the other. "We were too busy."

As they couldn't wonder or imagine anymore, they weren't sure how to solve the problem.

Chapter 5

Days turned into weeks and weeks turned
into months. Little Gumaan was crawling under
the trees. He listened to the breeze and to the birds.
He looked up at the night sky and imagined stories.
But he couldn't speak yet.

I looked up at the map, and then at the queen's face. As she sat down her anger flashed, and I finally understood why I'd been brought here. *He means they're discussing going to war,* I thought. *Maybe there's still time to stop it. There must be!* The ravens' warning had to have something to do with what was happening here.

I licked my lips and looked back at the king. "The ravens are sending us a message, Sire. They have been turning white. My father said you needed to know."

The king's eyes widened. "Turning white?"

I nodded.

The king began to speak again, but the queen interrupted him. "What is this superstitious nonsense? Get rid of this child and let us get on with our business!"

"Your Majesty," the king said, though his voice was stern. He turned to her. "I beg you to respect our customs. The ravens will be heard." He looked at me. "Where are the birds now?"

As he spoke, I heard the ravens' call. The shrieking, cackling chorus was enough to startle the queen. She got to her feet, and the king's guards tensed, as though ready to draw their swords.

The princess stood in front of her mother, her fists clenched, and then, through the door of the tent and every opening in its canvas, burst a flood of shining birds.

I heard the queen cry out, and the king shout that nobody was to harm the ravens, but everything else was a blur of silver light.

Chapter 7

Claws landed on my head and arms and the tent filled with a strange rustling, like trees in the wind. It only took a moment, and then the claws were gone, and the weight of the birds lifted away from me.

I looked down, and my breath caught in my neck. I was wearing a marvellous cloak made of sparkling feathers, long enough to sweep along the ground.

I looked at the princess. She was wearing a cloak too, identical to mine, and her eyes were wide with wonder.

"A white cloak," the queen murmured.

"The sign of truce," said the king, meeting her gaze.

I looked for my birds. They were perched all around the room, on every surface they could find, and they were black once more. They'd shaken out all their white feathers on the princess and me, and they looked exactly as they'd always done – except for Cuthbert, who had two white feathers left. The birds watched us with patient, gleaming eyes.

"Your Majesty," said the king, turning to the queen, "I propose a peaceful settlement to our dispute."

The queen gazed at her daughter. "I accept," she said.

After the negotiations were complete, and the battle
called off, the king made sure I had enough food to see
me home and the best horse that could be spared.

"Thank you," he said, looking up at my swirling birds.

Cuthbert fluttered to my shoulder, rummaging through his plumage with his long black beak. Finally, he found the two white feathers and pulled them free, holding them out. The king took them carefully, like they were treasure.

"Something to remember us by," I told him, and he smiled at me as he waved goodbye.

I rode away from the battlefield, following my birds. They were black as ink again, dark as soot, and it made me glad.

The horse made quick work of the journey, crossing the tumbling heather with long-legged ease and splashing through the gurgling beck, its water barely reaching her knees.

We stopped for the night by the same standing rock I'd sheltered under on my first journey over the moor, and by mid-morning the next day, the rookery tower came into view.

As soon as I saw it, I urged the horse to trot a little faster, until someone familiar came towards us, slow but steady, across the moor to meet me.

My father swept me off the horse and into his arms, and all around us, the air was filled with the ravens' joyful call. I was sure it sounded like a song.

45

Alys's journey

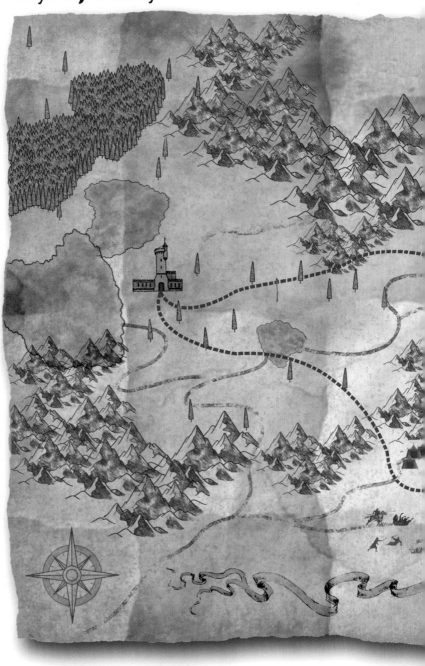

Ideas for reading

Written by Clare Dowdall, PhD

Lecturer and Primary Literacy Consultant

Reading objectives:
- discuss the sequence of events in books and how items of information are related
- become increasingly familiar with and retell a wider range of stories, fairy stories and traditional tales
- recognise simple recurring literary language in stories and poetry
- predict what might happen on the basis of what has been read so far

Spoken language objectives:
- give well-structured descriptions and explanations

- use spoken language to develop understanding through speculating, hypothesising, imagining and exploring ideas

Curriculum links: Art and design; Writing – composition

Word count: 2869

Interest words: apprentice, superstitious nonsense, settlement, dispute, plumage

Resources: ICT for research; paper and pencils; bird mask template, paper plates, glue and feathers

Build a context for reading

- Look at the front cover and read the title. Ask children to share anything that they know about ravens.

- Read the blurb to the children. Ask them to predict what will happen in this story, based on the information.

- Look closely at the image on the front cover. Discuss how the ravens are changing and whether this may be a message, or a warning.

Understand and apply reading strategies

- Read Chapter 1 around the group. Invite children to take a paragraph each. Support them to read aloud with fluency and expression.